IF WINNING ISN'T EVERYTHING, WHY DO I HATE TO LOSE?

Written by **BRYAN SMITH**

Illustrated by **BRIAN MARTIN**

If Winning Isn't Everything, Why Do I Hate To Lose?

Text and Illustrations Copyright © 2015 by Father Flanagan's Boys' Home
ISBN 978-1-934490-85-3

Published by the Boys Town Press
14100 Crawford St.
Boys Town, NE 68010

For a Boys Town Press catalog, call **1-800-282-6657**
or visit our website: **BoysTownPress.org**

Publisher's Cataloging-in-Publication Data

Smith, Bryan (Bryan Kyle), 1978-

If winning isn't everything, why do I hate to lose? / written by Bryan Smith ; illustrated by Brian Martin. -- Boys Town, NE : Boys Town Press, [2015]

pages : illustrations ; cm.

ISBN: 978-1-934490-85-3
Audience: grades K-6.
Summary: Kelsey is a sore loser and a sore winner. With help, however, she discovers that practicing good sportsmanship (or sportsGIRLship, as Kelsey likes to say) makes playing a lot more fun -- win or lose.--Publisher.

1. Sports--Psychological aspects--Juvenile fiction. 2. Success-- Psychological aspects--Juvenile fiction. 3. Failure (Psychology)--Juvenile fiction. 4. Sportsmanship--Juvenile fiction. 5. Children--Life skills guides-- Juvenile fiction. 6. [Winning and losing--Fiction. 7. Sports--Fiction. 8. Failure (Psychology)--Fiction. 9. Sportsmanship--Fiction. 10. Conduct of life--Fiction.] 11. Children's stories. I. Martin, Brian (Brian Michael), 1978- II. Title.

PZ7.S643366 I4 2015

[E]--dc23   1508

Printed in the United States
10 9 8 7 6 5 4 3 2

Boys Town Press is the publishing division of Boys Town, a national organization serving children and families.

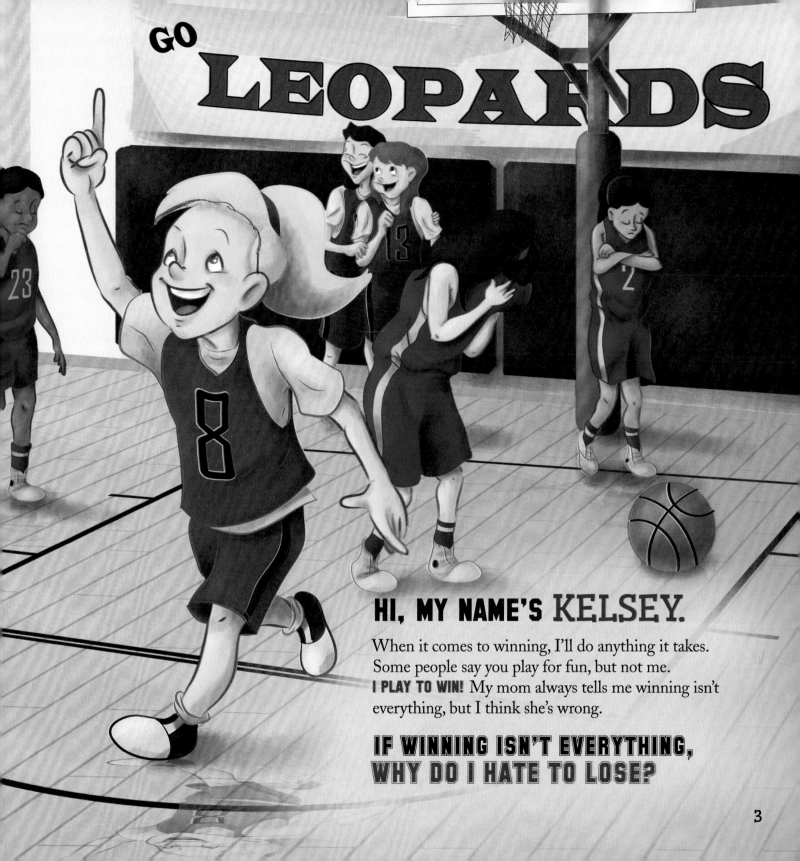

HI, MY NAME'S KELSEY.

When it comes to winning, I'll do anything it takes. Some people say you play for fun, but not me. **I PLAY TO WIN!** My mom always tells me winning isn't everything, but I think she's wrong.

IF WINNING ISN'T EVERYTHING, WHY DO I HATE TO LOSE?

My basketball team hadn't lost a game in like **FOREVER.** Of course, I'm the best player on the team, but we still have other girls who are pretty good. Last Friday, we were in a really close game. With 15 seconds left, we were up 40-39. A girl from the other team went up for a lay-up. Somehow, my hand grabbed her ponytail and yanked her to the ground.

OUCH!

I'm glad that wasn't my hair! I thought I got away with it, but the ref called me for a foul. The girl made both free throws, and her team went up by a point. Oh well, it was worth a try. My coach called a time-out.

I wondered what play he was going to call.

PLEASE, PLEASE, PLEASE

let me be the one to make the last shot!
I would be the hero, and they could carry
me off the court for winning the game.

Coach told all the girls where he wanted them to go. Well, that's weird. He never mentioned my name.

"Hey Coach, do you want me to take the last shot?"

"No, I want you to sit on the bench and I'm pretty sure you know why," he said.

Obviously, we ended up losing the game.

I pretended to feel sick so I wouldn't have to go shake hands with the other team. Afterwards, Coach told me to stick around because he wanted to talk.

"Kelsey, do you have any idea why I pulled you out?"

"Yeah, I guess you didn't want to win."

"Not true. You did something on purpose that needs to be addressed. You could have hurt that girl. When you cheat like that, you never win. Sure, your team may get more points than the other team, but that's still not winning!"

"**Cheat?!** What do you mean cheat? I didn't cheat! I just came up with a creative way to keep her from making that basket!" I said.

Coach looked at me and said, "It wasn't all that creative, it didn't keep her from getting the points anyway, and it **IS cheating**. Take a look at our Lady Leopards' Team Promises poster. You know, the promises all of you girls agreed to when you joined the team."

9

I looked up on the wall. Coach asked me to look at **#1, TRY YOUR HARDEST.**

I spoke up. "Coach, I DID try my hardest. I ALWAYS try my hardest!"

Coach said, "Kelsey, you played hard – most of the game. But I wonder, if you had focused more on defense instead of pulling that girl's hair, could you have stopped the ball?"

I thought about it for a second and just looked at him. "Maybe, but I don't know."

Coach said, "Right, you don't know. We'll never know. Because you didn't follow #2."

I looked up and saw **#2, DISPLAY GOOD SPORTSMANSHIP.**

"Kelsey, do you really think you displayed good sportsmanship?" Coach asked.

"SPORTSMANSHIP? That's not for me. I'm not a man, and I don't play sports in a ship." "No," Coach said. "You're not, and this is not a good time for silliness."

"Sportsmanship means you win and lose with class. That team beat us because they played a great game. That doesn't mean we didn't. We lost by a point. Both teams played well. They got more points. We shake their hands and tell them good game."

"Coach, I see what you're saying, but I think I'll call it 'SPORTSGirlSHIP.'"

He nodded and asked me to look at
#3, LEARN FROM YOUR MISTAKES.

"What did you learn from your mistake?"

I actually knew this answer. "Don't pull hair, play fair, and admit the other team won fair and square!"

"**That's a good first step,**" Coach said. "Take this card with our rules and keep it in your pocket as a reminder. Remember to use these rules here, at school, and at home. It's the best way to have fun!"

When I got home, I went to play Connect Four with my older brother, Anthony. It was my turn to go first, and things were going great. Well… for about thirty seconds. Before I knew it, he had me trapped. **NOT AGAIN!** There was only one thing I could do to keep from losing. I pretended to sneeze and knocked the game over.

"I hate playing with you," my brother said. "Don't you know cheaters never win?"

"I'm not a cheater, and at least I didn't lose."

Mom pulled me aside. "Kelsey, what you did was not an accident and was not part of the game, so it really is the same thing as cheating. And when you cheat, you actually lose, whether you get caught or not. Take a look at the card Coach gave you. Didn't he talk to you about **trying your hardest, winning and LOSING with class, and learning from your mistakes?**"

"Yeah."

"Kelsey, I saw that Anthony had you trapped. There really wasn't much you could do to keep from losing. But you should have kept trying your hardest. That's what #1 means: **TRY YOUR HARDEST!**"

"But Mom, it wouldn't have mattered. He had me trapped! I would have lost anyway."

"That may be the case. But then you should have just said 'Good game.' That's what #2 means: **DISPLAY GOOD SPORTSMANSHIP.**"

"But I just don't understand how he is able to trap me every time we play."

"Well, that sounds like a great question to ask him. And that is what #3 means: **LEARN FROM YOUR MISTAKES.**"

This whole **"SPORTSGirlSHIP"** thing was starting to make sense, even though it seemed like a lot of work. I told my brother I was sorry for knocking the game over and that he really won.

"Why don't you ever cheat? Don't you like winning?" I asked.

"Of course I do, but I want to know I actually won," Anthony said. **"If you cheat, you never know if you would have won fair and square."**

"How do you trap me all the time?" I asked.

He tried to hide it, but he was excited to show me. And so he did. It didn't seem too hard.

"Why didn't I think of that?" I said.

"Maybe because you were too busy thinking of ways to cheat?"

"Oh Yeah."

A while later, my little sister, Milly, asked me to play Connect Four. "Sure!" Now was my chance to try my new moves. She didn't even see it coming. I had her trapped like a bear in a cage at the zoo. She had nowhere to go to avoid losing the game.

I yelled out, **"CONNECT FOUR, IN YOUR FACE!"** She looked like she was going to cry. "Kelsey, seriously?" Mom said. "Come here. Remember how Coach said you should show good sportsmanship whether you're losing or WINNING? How is yelling at your sister showing good sportsmanship and winning with class?"

"I guess I could have said 'Good game,'" I mumbled.

"And maybe you could show her what Anthony taught you," Mom said.

"What? Then she might beat me!"

"Yes, she might. But how good would it feel to win even when she knew the trick? If you think about it, you might realize that **showing good sportsmanship feels a lot better.** It's the best way to have fun!"

"Okay, Mom. I'll apologize to Milly."

21

The next day at school was the true test. It was Field Day, and there were more than 20 events we could do. There was a small chance I might lose a few of them, so I tried to prepare myself for it. First was the sock hop.

On your mark, get set, FALL DOWN!

Just as the starter said "Go!" I tripped and fell flat on my face. I wanted to say someone tripped me and that we needed a restart, but I could see my teacher, Mr. Smith, watching me to see what I would do.

I started laughing and said,
"Did you all see that sack trip me?"

Mr. Smith said he loved how I had a positive attitude even though I didn't win. But he also said there was one more thing I should have done.

"But I didn't get mad at all!" I said.

"Yes, you're right, and that was fantastic! You can still go a step further. When someone else beats us fair and square, we should say…?"

"You know I let you win, right?" I said.

"Nice try but no," Mr. Smith said. "We still need to say

'GOOD GAME'

and shake the winner's hand. Try and remember this the rest of Field Day."

Next was the egg toss game. My partner and I won. The kids who lost came up to us and said, "Man, you guys were awesome!"

I told them, "You were great too."

You know, I guess you could say all of us had good **"SPORTSGirlSHIP"**!

The last event was the team relay race. I ran the first part of the race for my team and got us a huge lead right away. As the race went on, the other teams were getting closer and closer.

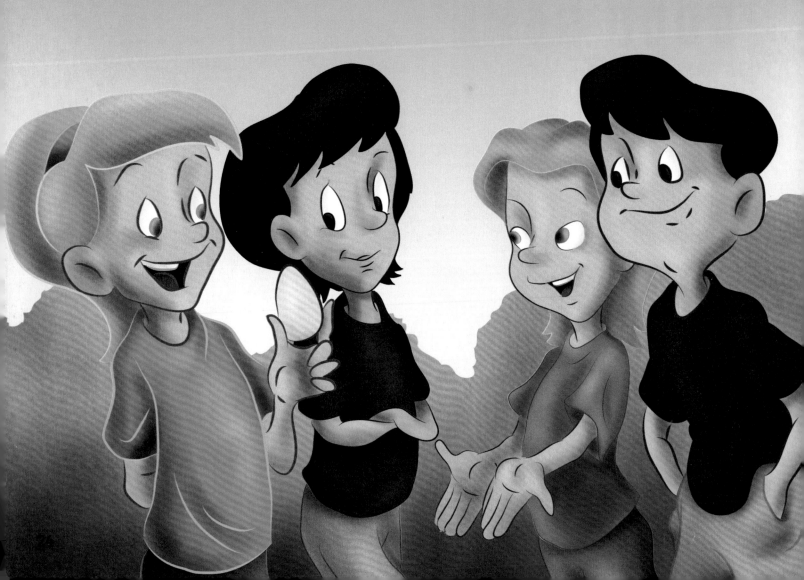

I was yelling, **"HURRY! HURRY! HURRY!"**
as each of my teammates ran their part of the race.
At the end, our runner and a runner from another team
were side-by-side as they crossed the finish line. Coach said
the other team won by an inch.

Now this story could have ended a few different ways. I could have said the other kids on my team lost the race for us since I gave them such a huge lead. I could have said Coach needed glasses because obviously it was a tie.

But I guess neither of those endings would have fit with the Lady Leopards' Team Promises.

So I walked over and gave everyone on the winning team a high-five and told them, **"Good race!"** Then I looked around. There was still one thing I needed to do.

I went over to the kids on my team and said, **"Good try. Maybe next time."**

The other kids said, "We thought you were going to be mad at us for losing."

"We didn't lose," I said. "It's just that our team didn't win. We win as a team and lose as one. And I guess it really doesn't matter whether we win or lose. The most important part is that we

WORK HARD, MAKE SURE WE HAVE GOOD 'SPORTSGIRLSHIP,' AND LEARN FROM OUR MISTAKES.

It's the best way to have fun! And I say we're winners at that!"

When I left school that day, I felt good inside. I was excited to tell Mom about everything that happened. And I was even more excited to tell her about the times when I didn't win. I might even tell her she was right.

WINNING ISN'T EVERYTHING.

It still feels better than losing, but I guess I don't HATE losing quite as much anymore.

It's normal for kids to WANT TO WIN and to STRUGGLE WHEN THEY LOSE.

How children react to losing may vary from being slightly disappointed to displaying more extreme reactions, like throwing a tantrum! Whether kids experience winning or losing, such situations offer great opportunities for teachers and parents to use these teaching tips:

- When your child loses at any game, be sure to **point out the positives** of how he or she reacted (gave best effort, never quit trying, shook hands with opponents, etc.).

- **After a game** (whether it was a win or a loss), ask your child to name one thing he or she did really well and one thing that could be improved.

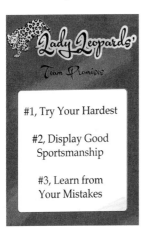

Lady Leopards'
Team Promises

#1, Try Your Hardest

#2, Display Good Sportsmanship

#3, Learn from Your Mistakes

- **Have your child ask other family members** what they think good sportsmanship means. Discuss the different responses with your child.

- **When attending** any sporting event, be sure to point out any examples of good or bad sportsmanship.

- Teach your child to **treat others the way he or she wants to be treated.** This can help reinforce the concept of empathy.

- Make it a point **not to show frustration** over your child's mistakes during a game. It can have a negative effect on his or her performance.

- Explain to your child that it is **okay to make mistakes,** and the only thing you ask is that he or she learns from them.

- Make sure your child always **supports his or her teammates,** whether he or she is playing in the game or sitting on the bench.

- Most importantly, remind your child that **playing any game is supposed to be fun** and that winning or losing badly takes away the fun for everyone!

For more parenting information, visit boystown.org/parenting.

BOYS TOWN
Parenting

31

Boys Town Press Featured Titles
Kid-friendly books to teach social skills

Executive FuNction

What Were You Thinking?
Written by Bryan Smith
Illustrated by Lisa M. Griffin

978-1-934490-85-3

Downloadable Activities
Go to BoysTownPress.org
to download.

My Day Is Ruined!
A Story for Teaching Flexible Thinking
Written by Bryan Smith
Illustrated by Lisa M. Griffin

978-1-944882-04-4

Of COURSE It's a Big Deal!
A Story about Learning to React Calmly and Appropriately
Written by Bryan Smith
Illustrated by Lisa M. Griffin

978-1-944882-11-2

MINDSET MATTERS
Written by Bryan Smith
Illustrated by Lisa Griffin

978-1-944882-12-9

Is There an App for That?
Written by Bryan Smith
Illustrated by Kelsi Wish

Hailey Discovers HAPPiness through Self-Acceptance

978-1-934490-74-7

Is There an App for That?
Activity Guide
Written by Bryan Smith
Illustrated by Kelsi Wish

Lessons to Teach and Reinforce Self-Acceptance and Positive Changes

978-1-934490-75-4

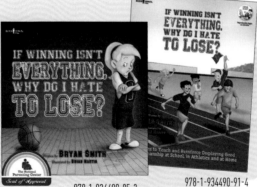

IF WINNING ISN'T EVERYTHING, WHY DO I HATE TO LOSE?
BRYAN SMITH
Illustrated by Brian Martin

978-1-934490-85-3

IF WINNING ISN'T EVERYTHING, WHY DO I HATE TO LOSE?
Lessons to Teach and Reinforce Displaying Good Sportsmanship at School, in Athletics and at Home

978-1-934490-91-4

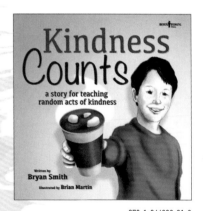

Kindness Counts
a story for teaching random acts of kindness
Written by Bryan Smith
Illustrated by Brian Martin

978-1-944882-01-3

Downloadable Activities
Go to BoysTownPress.org to download.

BOYS TOWN® Press

For information on Boys Town, its Education Model, Common Sense Parenting®, and training programs:
boystowntraining.org | boystown.org/parenting
training@BoysTown.org | 1-800-545-5771

For parenting and educational books and other resources:
BoysTownPress.org
btpress@BoysTown.org | 1-800-282-6657